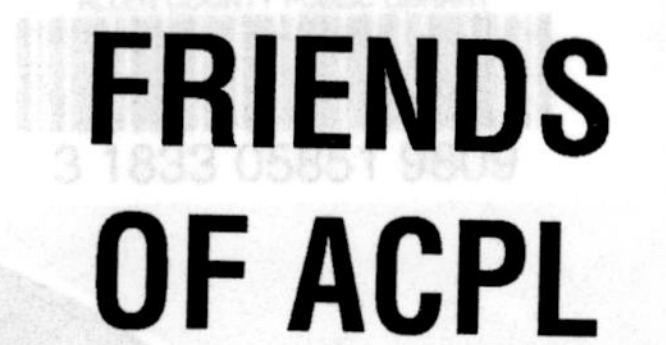

Rosa M. Curto / Aleix Cabrera

The fairies tell us about... Compassion

BARRON'S

On the other side of the Enchanted Forest, there was a pond full of green and brown frogs that croaked and jumped endlessly. The sight delighted an old raccoon named Binks. That's why he went there early in the morning and stayed until the sun set.

3

The path was not easy and Binks could no longer see or smell as he had when he was young. He needed somebody to be his guide. Belle the fairy had always looked after him and had never let him down … except for that afternoon. Where was she?

At the apple tree festival, all the fairies had gotten bellyaches from eating cakes, forest fruits, and drinking a delicious apple juice with cinnamon. Belle, who wasn't used to eating so much, felt sleepy and laid down to rest on her way to the pond.

By the time the fairy woke up, it was already night.
She was very frightened when she remembered her
old friend. What will have become of the raccoon?
Will he have gone home alone?
And what if he got lost?

Belle thought that she had let her friend down.
She was upset, but above all, angry with herself.
And when a fairy is sad or angry, she can't make
her body glow no matter how hard she tries.

It was so dark that the fairy was tripping over her own feet. But if she flew, she would bump into the branches. She started to cry.

"What's wrong? Can I help you?" someone said.

Belle lifted up her head and saw a nice insect on a tree.

"Yes, please, help me get to the pond," begged the fairy. "But how will you do it? You're only a bug..."

“Don’t let yourself be fooled by what you see,” he said with a smile. “Your eyes and mind can trick you. I’m Twinkle, a special bug. Explain to me what your path looks like and I’ll try to help you.”

In the midst of sobs and cries,
Belle remembered that to go to
the pond, she always went
through a field of poppies...,

... turned right at the
loving fir trees...,

... caught her breath at the holey rock and splashed in the mimosa stream.

Then she followed the stream.

"I have friends in all of those places," said Twinkle in a happy voice. "Now be quiet! I have to concentrate."

Twinkle closed his eyes and moved his antenna from side to side.

Suddenly, the forest was lit up by small glowing yellow, green, and red circles. "You're a glow worm!" cried out the fairy.

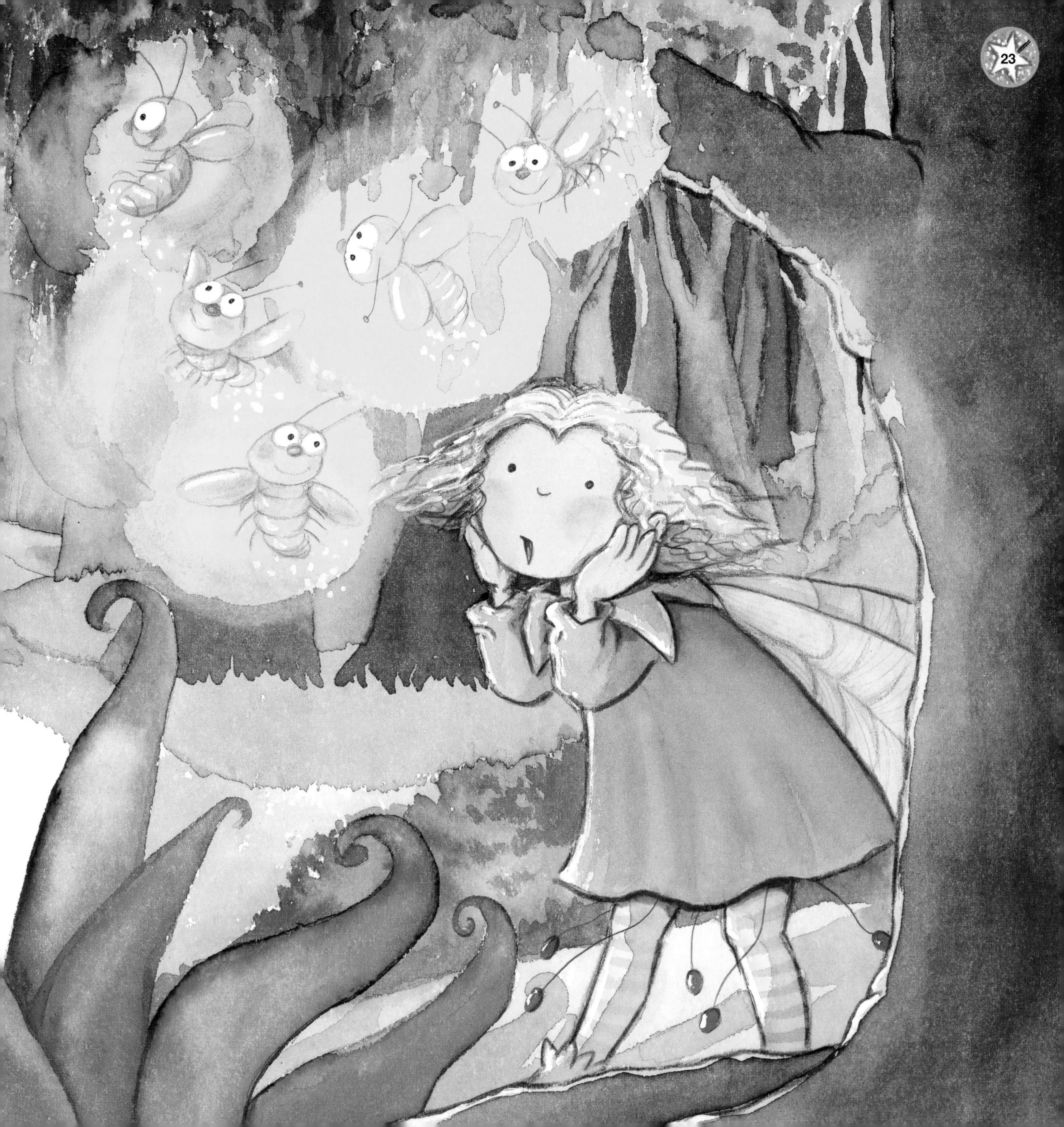

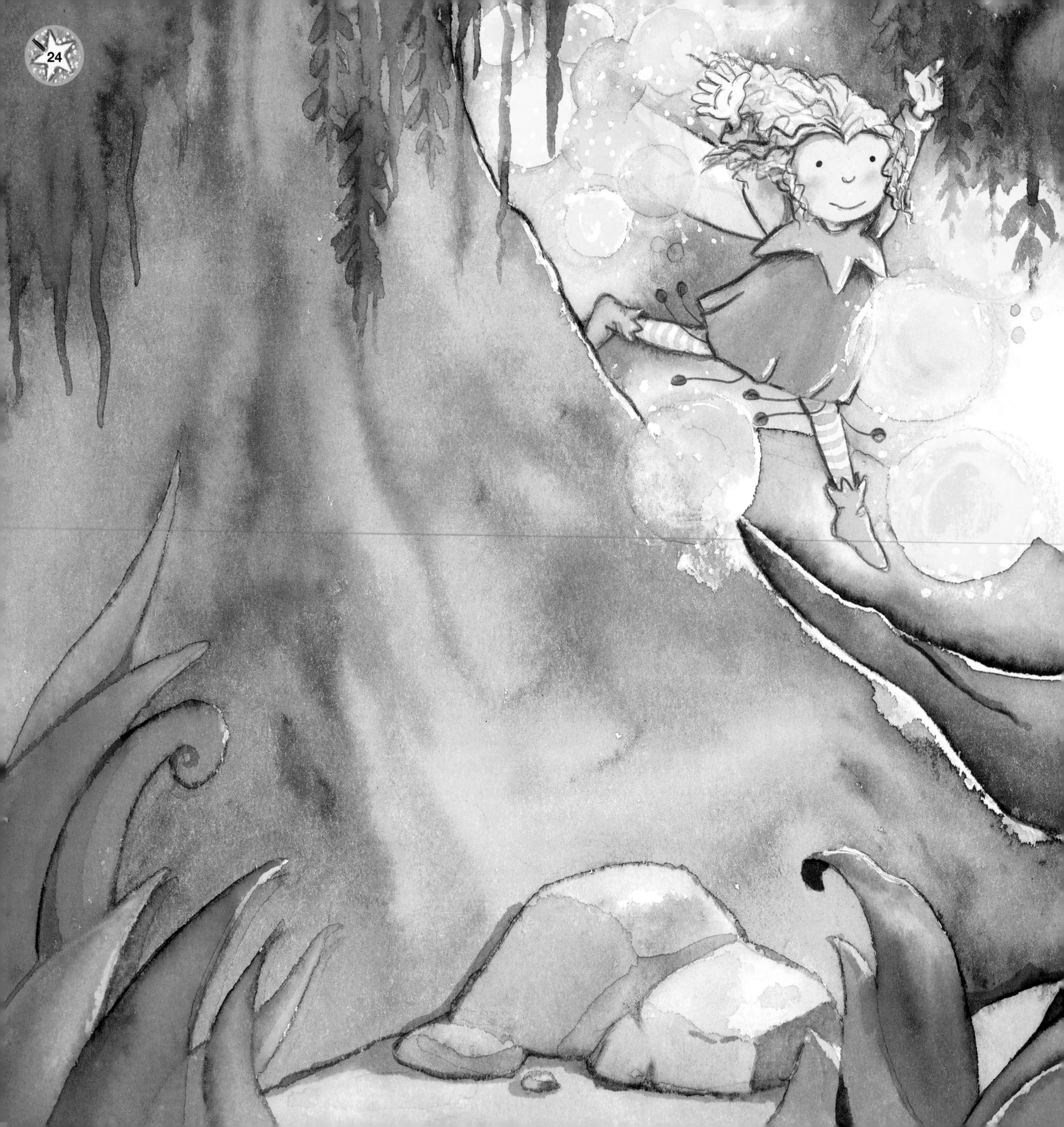

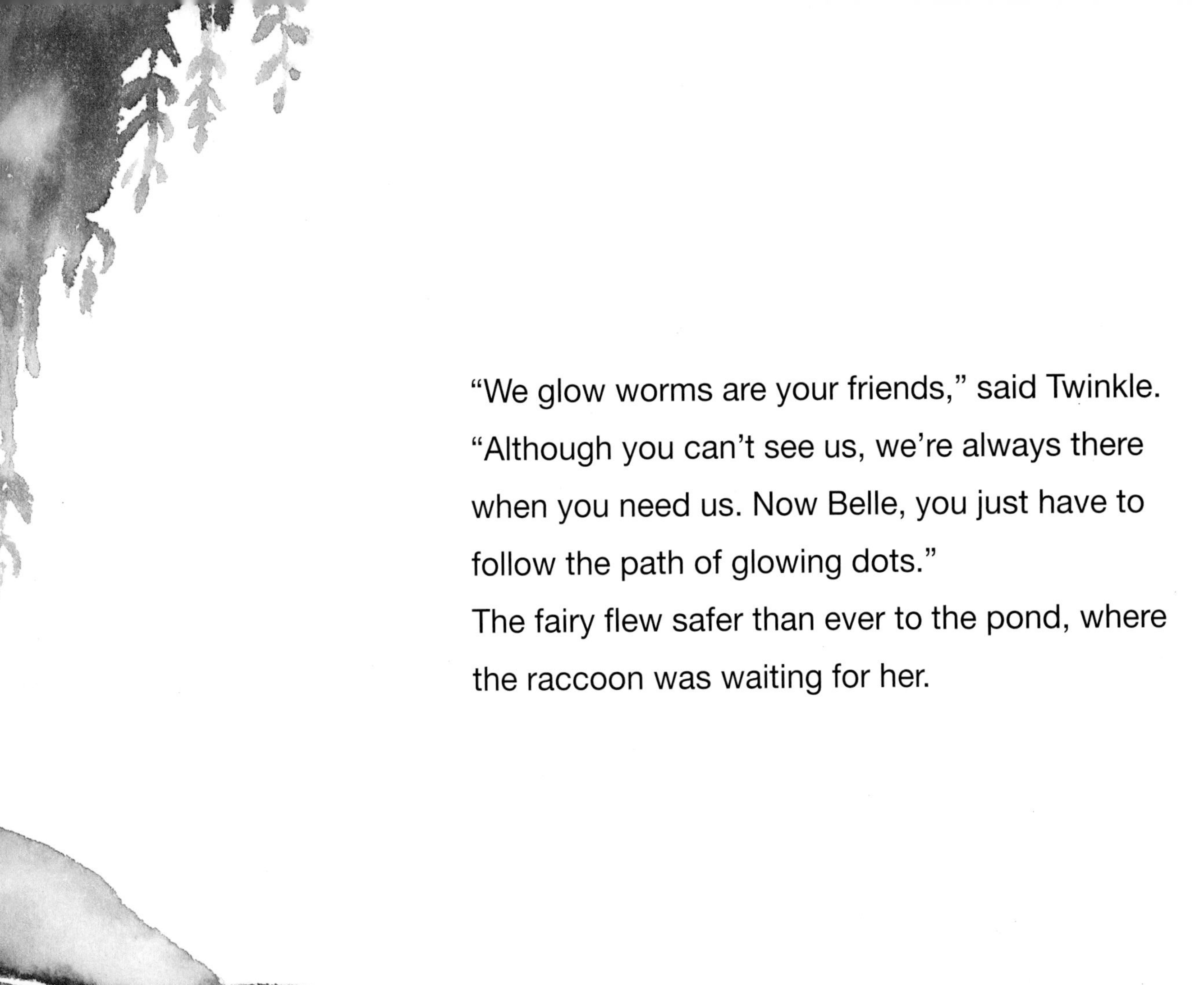

"We glow worms are your friends," said Twinkle. "Although you can't see us, we're always there when you need us. Now Belle, you just have to follow the path of glowing dots."

The fairy flew safer than ever to the pond, where the raccoon was waiting for her.

Belle explained to Binks that like him, she needed help to find him. Now she understood how her friend felt and how much she meant to him. She had put herself in his place and it brought them even closer.

Learning more

The fairy house

Fairies everywhere

There are as many houses in the world as there are fairies. Most of them prefer to live in high places, hidden from the wind and rain, rather than living close to the ground and in cold, wet places.

Some city fairies live in church towers, close to the storks, because they can see everything from up there. They also like mouse holes, cracks in walls, and lofts, where they often leave their mark.

In the forest and the jungle, many fairies like to sleep inside perfumed flowers. Others sleep on large leaves or hammocks built among the reeds. The water fairies prefer to hide behind waterfalls or inside empty snail and sea shells.

The forest animals...

Just like the fairies, the forest animals also choose different places to live, depending on what they need.

Houses in the trees

Many birds build their nests in the treetops and some of them spend more time in it than others. Finches use different materials for each of the three layers: moss and spiders' webs for the outside; more moss and mud for the middle layer; and hair, feathers, and wool for the inside. On the other hand, the magpie uses small branches and builds more than one nest in the same tree, although she only lays eggs in one of them. The squirrel also lives in the trees. This rodent makes use of holes in the trunk and gathers branches to make its home.

A hiding place underground

Some animals are natural burrowers and they actually make homes underground to live. They range from invertebrates, like worms, ants, and crickets that live in small holes, to mammals, like mice, rabbits, and moles. The groundhog even covers the exit with hay before hibernating, when the cold weather arrives. You wouldn't dream of waking him up!

Hedgehogs also hibernate and they prefer to take cover from the weather in a nest of dry grass. Nearby, you might find a snake and some small bugs like spiders and scorpions. A lot of bugs hide underneath rocks and tree trunks and they don't all die in winter. Some enter into a state of hibernation called diapause, like butterflies, for example.

... and their places to live

Mountains and water

The rocky places in the mountains are a favorite place for some mammals, like mountain goats and birds of prey, such as eagles and vultures. In the depths of the rocks, in natural caves, bears and bats seek shelter—as they love darkness and humidity.

Aquatic birds such as coots sometimes build floating nests anchored to the shore reeds. And below them, live a large variety of aquatic insects, fish, and amphibians.

But not all animals build their own houses. There is one that always carries it with him. Do you know which one it is?
Can you find it in this picture?

Compassion

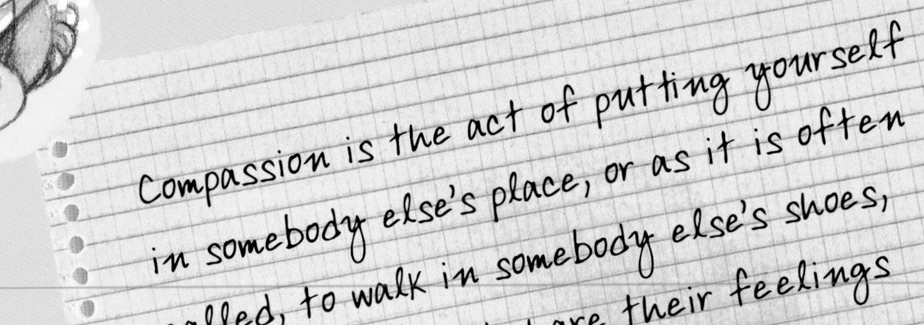

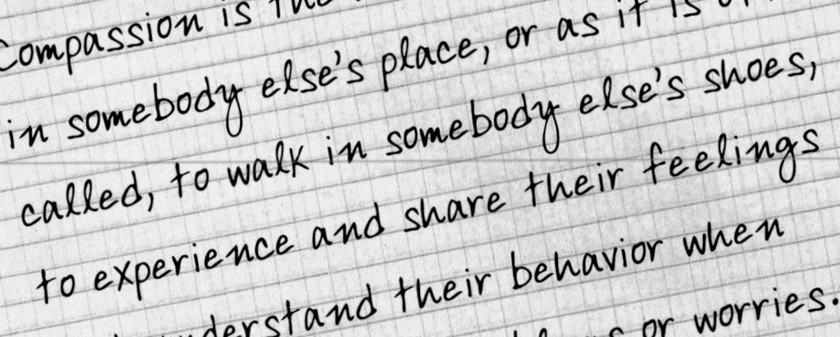

Compassion is the act of putting yourself in somebody else's place, or as it is often called, to walk in somebody else's shoes, to experience and share their feelings and understand their behavior when faced with certain problems or worries.

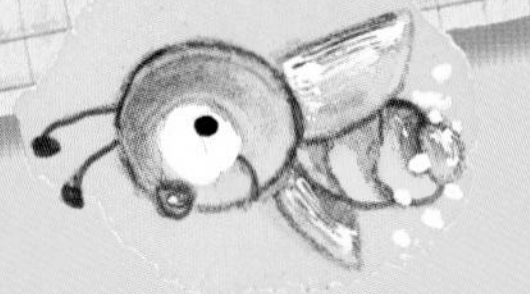

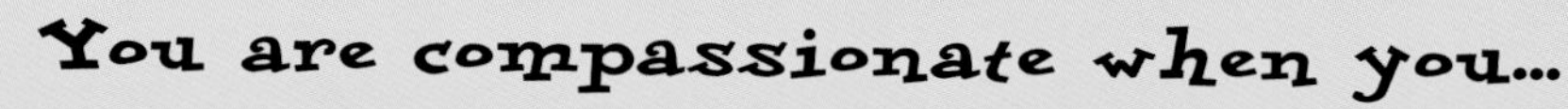

You are compassionate when you...

try to understand another person's behavior, even when you don't agree, feel sad because someone else is sad, or feel like laughing when a friend is happy.

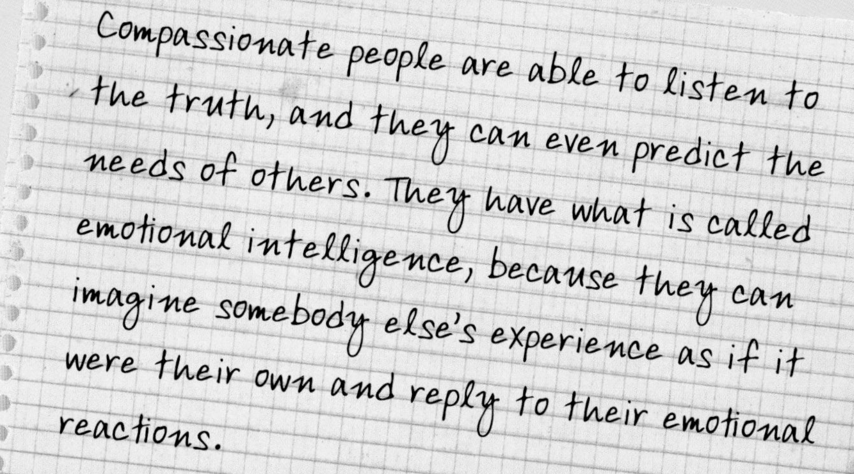
Compassionate people are able to listen to the truth, and they can even predict the needs of others. They have what is called emotional intelligence, because they can imagine somebody else's experience as if it were their own and reply to their emotional reactions.

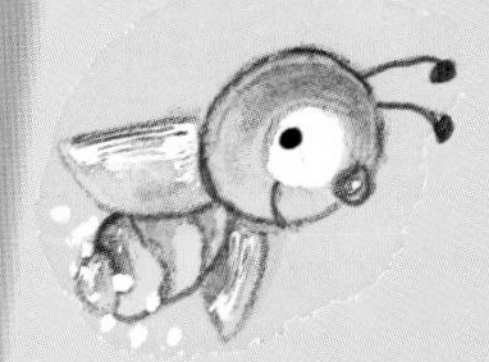

In the story, Twinkle shows compassion for Belle the fairy when he listens to her problem and tries to help her. But when the adventure is over, Belle is also able to put herself in the raccoon's place, because she has experienced a similar situation: She needed to be guided by somebody.

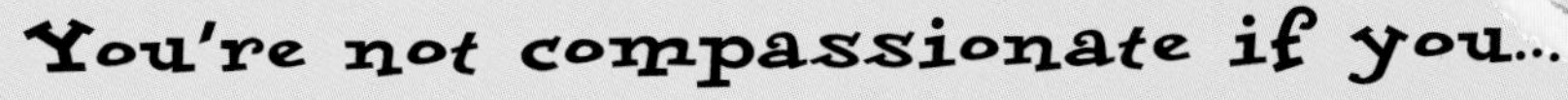

You're not compassionate if you...

think about your own worries while somebody is talking to you.

Only think about your needs.

Don't put yourself in the other person's shoes to understand their problems.

The fairies tell us about...
Compassion

Author: **Aleix Cabrera**
Illustrations: **Rosa M. Curto**
Design and layout: **Gemser Publications, S.L.**

First edition for the United States and Canada
published in 2010 by Barron's Educational Series, Inc.

El Castell, 38 08329 Teià (Barcelona, Spain)

All inquiries should be addressed to:
Barron's Educational Series, Inc.
250 Wireless Boulevard
Hauppauge, New York 11788
http: //www.barronseduc.com

ISBN-13: 978-0-7641-4375-5
ISBN-10: 0-7641-4375-1

Library of Congress Control No. 2009934836

Printed in China by L. Rex Printing Company Limited
Manufactured December 2009

9 8 7 6 5 4 3 2 1